Five reasons why we t... you'll love this book!

Winnie AND Wilbur
THE MIDNIGHT DRAGON

This book is so funny, even the portraits on Winnie's wall are laughing!

No dragons were harmed in the making of this book!

There is so much to spot in every picture.

You'll love Winnie's toothbrush!

You can take the Winnie and Wilbur challenge: how many moons can you count?

Freya

Anushka

Maggie

Bailey

Johannes

Molly

Ashley

Amber

Jun-Yeong

Pablo

Matilda

Marwin

Hasan

Rebecca

Thank you to all these schools for helping with the endpapers:

St Barnabas Primary School, Oxford; St Ebbe's Primary School, Oxford; Marcham Primary School, Abingdon; St Michael's C.E. Aided Primary School, Oxford; St Bede's RC Primary School, Jarrow; The Western Academy, Beijing, China; John King School, Pinxton; Neston Primary School, Neston; Star of the Sea RC Primary School, Whitley Bay; José Jorge Letria Primary School, Cascais, Portugal; Dunmore Primary School, Abingdon; Özel Bahçeşehir İlköğretim Okulu, Istanbul, Turkey; the International School of Amsterdam, the Netherlands; Princethorpe Infant School, Birmingham.

For Jenny and Louise in Canada—V.T.

For Sue Matthew—K.P.

OXFORD
UNIVERSITY PRESS

Great Clarendon Street, Oxford OX2 6DP

Oxford University Press is a department of the University of Oxford. It furthers the University's objective of excellence in research, scholarship, and education by publishing worldwide. Oxford is a registered trade mark of Oxford University Press in the UK and in certain other countries

Text copyright © Valerie Thomas 2006
Illustrations copyright © Korky Paul 2006, 2016
The moral rights of the author and artist have been asserted

Database right Oxford University Press (maker)

First published as *Winnie's Midnight Dragon* in 2006
This edition first published in 2016

British Library Cataloguing in Publication Data available

ISBN: 978-0-19-274823-2 (paperback)
ISBN: 978-0-19-274909-3 (paperback and CD)

10 9 8 7 6 5 4 3 2 1

Printed in China

Paper used in the production of this book is a natural, recyclable product made from wood grown in sustainable forests. The manufacturing process conforms to the environmental regulations of the country of origin

www.winnieandwilbur.com

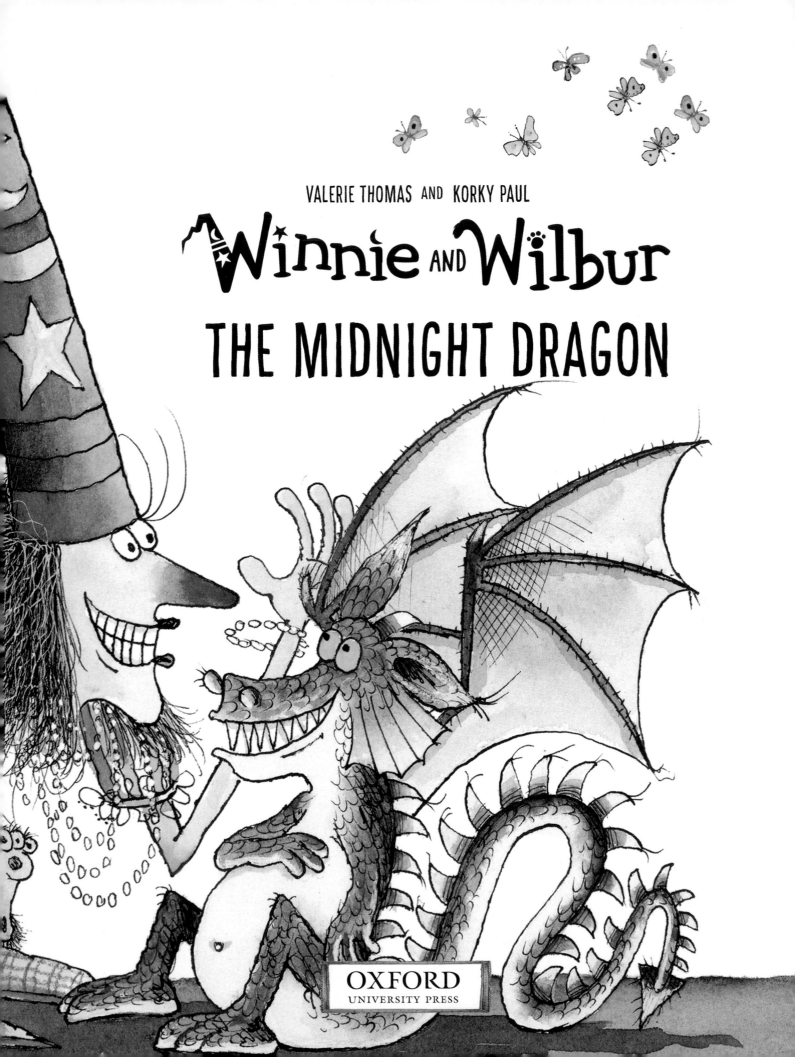

VALERIE THOMAS AND KORKY PAUL

Winnie and Wilbur
THE MIDNIGHT DRAGON

OXFORD
UNIVERSITY PRESS

'Time for bed,' said Winnie the Witch,
    as the clock struck twelve.
Witches always go to bed at midnight.
Winnie turned off the lights and went upstairs.

She brushed her teeth, washed her face,
put on her nightie and climbed into bed.
In two minutes she was snoring.

Wilbur, her big black cat, was already asleep.
He was curled up in his basket, dreaming.

Two minutes later, Wilbur woke up.
He could hear a funny noise in the garden.

He crept to the cat flap and peeped out.
There was something on the door mat.
Something with big green eyes.

'Meeoww!' cried Wilbur
and he jumped back.
A long nose poked
through the cat flap.

Then there was a puff of smoke.
The cat flap wobbled and shook.

A spiky body, then a long tail, followed the nose.
There was a baby dragon in Winnie's house!
'Meeoww!' cried Wilbur. He turned three
backward somersaults and ran into the hall.

The baby dragon thought this was fun.
He ran after Wilbur.
Swish, swish went his tail.
Winnie's grandfather clock wobbled and shook.

DING!   DONG!   BOING!

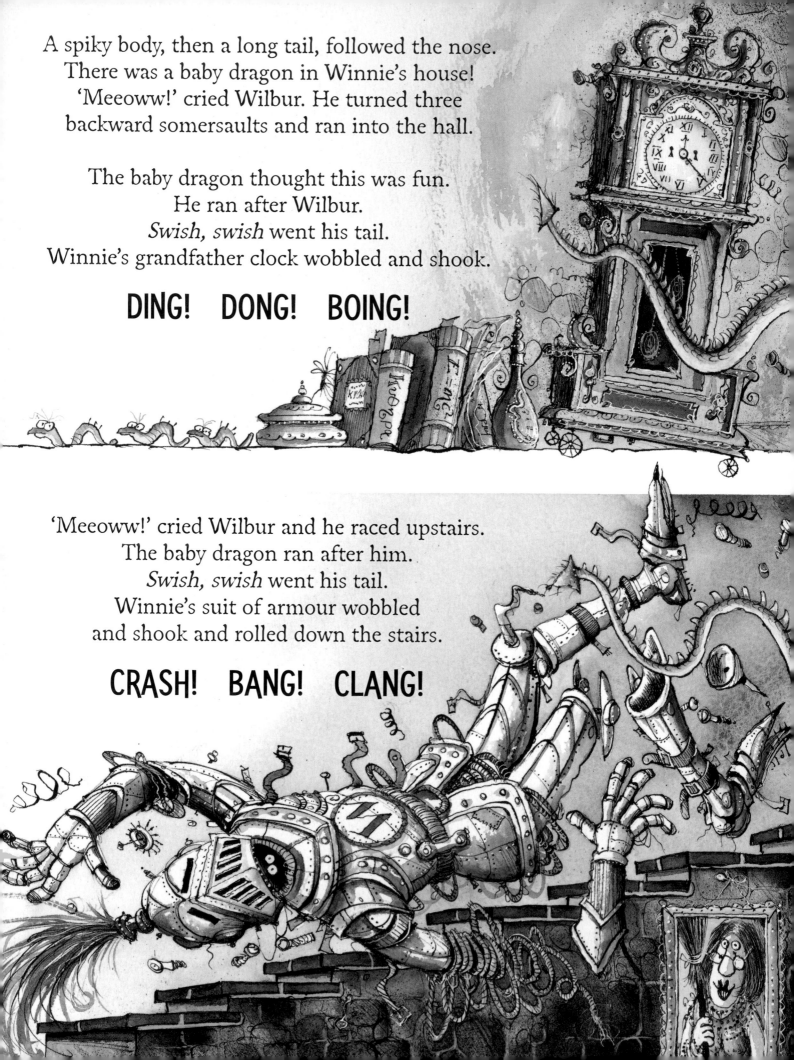

'Meeoww!' cried Wilbur and he raced upstairs.
The baby dragon ran after him.
Swish, swish went his tail.
Winnie's suit of armour wobbled
and shook and rolled down the stairs.

CRASH!   BANG!   CLANG!

'Meeoww!' cried Wilbur outside Winnie's door.
Winnie woke up and jumped out of bed.
'Whatever's that?' she said.

Then she saw a puff of smoke coming
from behind her broomstick.
'Oh no!' said Winnie. 'My broomstick is on fire!'

Winnie grabbed her broomstick.
'Goodness gracious me!' said Winnie.
'It's a baby dragon! He could burn my house down.
We'll have to find his mother, Wilbur.'

'Where's your mother, little dragon?'
Winnie asked.
'Boo hoo hoo,' cried the baby dragon.

A cloud of smoke came out of his nose.
Puff, puff.

Then Winnie had an idea.
She waved her magic wand three times, and shouted,

'Abracadabra!'

'Puff!' went the dragon,
and out of his nose came . . .

a cloud of butterflies.
'Puff, puff, puff,' went the baby dragon,
who was very surprised.

SMASH!
went Winnie's best bowl.

SPLASH!
went the vase of flowers.

There were butterflies everywhere.
Wilbur loved chasing butterflies.
The baby dragon loved chasing anything!

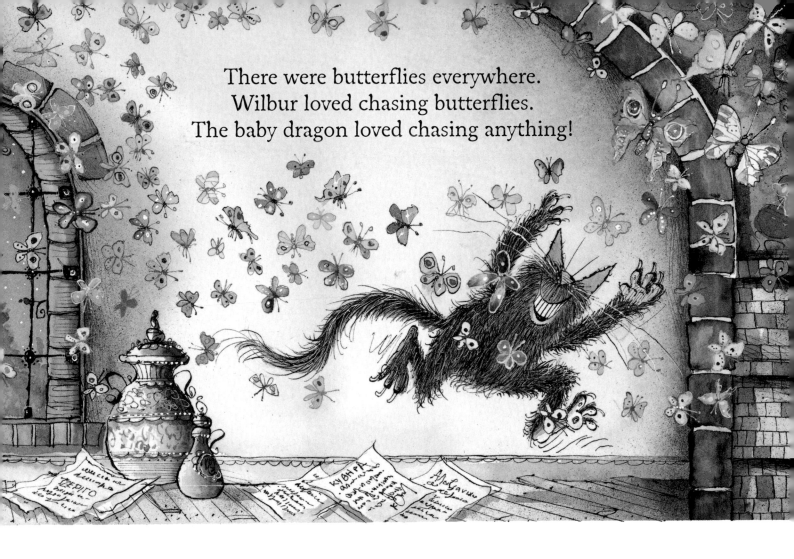

CRASH!
went the table.

'That wasn't such a good idea,' said Winnie.
She waved her magic wand again, and shouted,
'Abracadabra!'

Out of the dragon's nose came . . .
Nothing.

'Good,' said Winnie. 'Now let's get some sleep.'
But the baby dragon didn't want to sleep.
He wanted to play.

'Bother!' said Winnie.
'We'd better find your mother right now!'

She got a torch and went out onto the roof.
'Yoo hoo,' she called.

It was quiet and dark on the roof.
'Yoo hoo,' Winnie called again,
and waved her torch.

Suddenly there was a flash of fire,
and the sound of great wings.
The baby dragon jumped up and down.
'Mamamamama,' he called.
'Yoo hoo hoo!' called Winnie.

But the baby dragon's mother didn't see them.
Then Winnie had a wonderful idea.

She grabbed her wand,
waved it six times, shouted,

'Abracadabra!'
and there, above her house,
was an enormous moon.

The mother dragon came flying back.
She swooped down and scooped up her baby.

'Wait a minute!' called Winnie.
She waved her magic wand, and shouted,

'Abracadabra!'

'Puff!' went the baby dragon and smoke
came out of his nose again.

The two dragons flew high into the sky and disappeared.

Winnie waved her wand, shouted,

'Abracadabra!'

and the enormous moon went out.
'Now let's go back to bed, Wilbur,' she said.

Winnie climbed into bed and shut her eyes.
In half a minute she was snoring.
Wilbur was already asleep in his basket.

Just then, the sun rose. The night was over.
But Winnie the Witch and Wilbur were fast asleep.

Bethany

Katia

Eun-Jae

Kathleen

Ji-Eun

Jenny

Sara

Fraser

Ka Keung

Selin

Selin

Olivia

Siyabend

Kieran

A note for grown-ups

Oxford Owl is a FREE and easy-to-use website packed with support and advice about everything to do with reading.

Informative videos

Hints, tips and fun activities

Top tips from top writers for reading with your child

Help with choosing picture books

For this expert advice and much, much more about how children learn to read and how to keep them reading ...

LOOK
for Oxford Owl
www.oxfordowl.co.uk